Robin Hood

The Robin Hood stories have thrilled
children for hundreds of years, but there
is always room for a new interpretation.
Edward Blishen has based his five tales
on the old ballads, and shows a little
of the true background as well as
the excitement of the adventures. The
book begins with Earl Robert's flight to
the greenwood on his wedding day, tells
how his famous band was formed and how
his men lived, and ends with the return
of King Richard from the crusades,
and Robin's welcome back to court.

The stories were told on *Jackanory*
by Gilbert Wynne.

ROBIN HOOD

Edward Blishen

as told on Jackanory
by Gilbert Wynne

Illustrated by Graham McCallum

British Broadcasting Corporation

Published by the British Broadcasting Corporation
35 Marylebone High Street, London W1M 4AA

SBN: 563 08462 6

First published 1969, reprinted 1974, 1976

Text © Edward Blishen 1969, illustrations © BBC 1969

Printed in England by Cox & Wyman Ltd,
London, Reading and Fakenham

1

Come listen to me you gallants so free
All you that of mirth love to hear,
And I will tell you of a bold outlaw
That lived in Nottinghamshire.

That bold outlaw who lived in Nottingham-shire was the most famous outlaw the world has ever known, and his name was Robin Hood. It all happened a long time ago, when Richard I was King of England, and when the countryside was much more wild than it is today. There were few towns, and those were small. There were no great highways, and everywhere there were enormous forests full of deer belonging to the king.

But King Richard was not in England. He was far away, fighting in the Crusades, and he had left England in the care of the Bishop of Ely. But Richard had a brother, Prince John, a cruel and greedy man, who had driven out the Bishop, and ruled England for himself and his followers. And his followers were as greedy as he was. One way they made money was to accuse some rich man of breaking the law, and then take his land for themselves, while he became an outlaw, hiding in the forests.

Nor was it only the rich who suffered. The poor too – if they killed the king's deer or supported King Richard – often became outlaws. Then they too would hide in the forest, getting to know its secret paths, living by hunting the deer, and waiting for the day when King Richard would come home.

But when John heard of men who were loyal to his brother and willing to wait for his return, he laughed. For it was said that

King Richard had been made a prisoner on his way back from Jerusalem: no one knew where, nor if he would ever escape. "We're safe enough," said Prince John, "he'll not come back," and the Sheriff of Nottingham joined in his laughter. For John was staying in the Sheriff's castle that night, being entertained with a great feast.

When the feast was at its merriest, a man suddenly burst into the hall and threw himself on his knees before the high table.

"My Lords," said he, "I'm steward to

Robert Fitzooth, Earl of Huntingdon . . ."

"Fitzooth!" exclaimed the Prince. "*He's* not Earl of Huntingdon! One of my men is Earl of Huntingdon! What does this mean, Sheriff?"

"I know, My Lord, that you've driven out the Fitzooths," said the Sheriff, "but the people round here still call Robert Fitzooth their Lord."

"Their Lord!" cried Prince John. "I'll show them who is their lord."

"I came to tell you," said the man on his knees, "that tomorrow my master is to be married. Tonight he is holding a great feast in his castle at Locksley, which he still has, and all are welcome. If you were to come in disguise, My Lords, you'd hear my master speak of King Richard, and how all will be well when the King comes home."

"Yes," said the Sheriff, "and he'll talk of Robin Hood too, I dare say."

"Robin Hood!" said Prince John, white

with anger. "I've heard of Robin Hood. He lives in this forest of yours, and helps my enemies and robs my friends. And he robs me too, by killing my deer . . ."

"Yes," said the man on his knees, "he kills the king's deer . . ."

"*My* deer," said Prince John. "Come, Sheriff! If this Robert Fitzooth is a friend of Robin Hood and is true to King Richard, then he is my enemy and I will be rid of him. We shall be at his feast tonight, and hear what we shall hear."

So Prince John and the Sheriff of Nottingham went to Locksley castle in disguise. What they heard was enough for Prince John, and for the Sheriff too – they knew this Robin Fitzooth was no friend of theirs. As they rode back to the castle at Nottingham, they made a plan. And as soon as they arrived, they sent for a friend of theirs – Sir Guy of Gisborne.

It was the next morning – the morning

that Robert Fitzooth was going to be
married. Along the forest paths to the church
came Robert and his bowmen. And though
they came for a wedding, they carried their
bows.

"Armed for a wedding!" cried Lord
Fitzwalter, the father of Lady Marian, the
bride.

"Armed for a wedding!" cried the fat
Abbot, who was to conduct the service.

But Earl Robert's men went into the

church and stood quietly waiting. They
threw back their hoods, for they were in
church, but still they looked as though they'd
come for a battle, not a wedding. The Abbot
didn't like it, but he began the service. Lady
Marian smiled and Earl Robert smiled as
they stood together in front of the Abbot.
The monks chanted, and the church was
peaceful, for all those lines of armed men.
Until there was a sudden clatter of hooves
outside, a clash and clang of armour, and in

strode a knight, sword in hand. Behind him came a line of men in chain mail, as though ready for battle.

"I am Sir Guy of Gisborne," said the knight. "In the name of Prince John, ruler of England, I order that this wedding shall go no further. And I also declare that Robert Fitzooth, who calls himself Earl of Huntingdon, is none other than the traitor and outlaw Robin Hood!"

"Robin Hood!" cried the monks.

"Robin Hood!" cried the fat Abbot.

"His lands must be taken from him," the knight shouted, "and he must become my prisoner!"

The peace of the church was shattered. Earl Robert's men had their hands on their bows, and Earl Robert faced Sir Guy. "Sir Guy," said he, "I am no traitor. I am loyal to my true king, King Richard. It is not he, and it is not any who are faithful to him, who have sent you here. How you

13

discovered I am Robin Hood I cannot tell."

Earl Robert looked hard at Sir Guy, as if he expected an answer. But Sir Guy said nothing about the visit that Prince John and the Sheriff, disguised, had made to Locksley the night before; or of the things they'd heard whispered that had made them certain that Earl Robert was Robin Hood.

"But I *am* Robin Hood," said Earl Robert, "and now, until our true king returns, I shall be Earl Robert no longer. I and my followers will live in Sherwood Forest, and there shall be war between us and you. There shall be war on those who grow fat while the poor grow thin: on abbots and bishops who rob the poor, on false knights and false sheriffs and princes untrue to the king, on all who are cruel and all who do wrong, and I shall be Robin Hood till King Richard is back in England."

There was a cry from Lady Marian, and Robert turned to her and said:

"My Lady, I know you gave your love to Earl Robert; will you give it to Robin Hood?"

"Earl or outlaw, I will be your wife," said Lady Marian.

Then Robert said to her father: "Take Lady Marian, and take good care of her. Half a wedding we've had today, the whole of a wedding we'll have when King Richard's home!"

And then, as Lord Fitzwalter took his daughter out of the church, hands clutched tighter at bows and swords, and the monks and the abbot fled.

Sir Guy stepped forward. "Give yourself up," he cried. "You cannot escape, Robin Hood! Give up your sword and yourself!"

"Give up my sword!" said Robert, lifting it high. "Here it is! Take it!" and he brought it down on Sir Guy's helmet. Sir Guy fell at his feet, and now, with his men behind him cheering, Robert strode forward and the fight began. It was Lincoln green against grey armour, sword against sword, and a rain of arrows. Where, such a short time before, there had been the chanting of the monks, now there was the fierce sound of arrows flying, a groan, a cry, a cheer. And then, with his men, Robert was at the door of the church and out of it. A few paces, and green swallowed green: the green of the forest swallowed the outlaw and his bowmen together.

When Sir Guy recovered his wits, and got to his feet shaking with rage, all he saw outside the church was the forest, with the trees shining in the morning sun. And all he heard was the sound of a horn, a high ringing sound that seemed to be mocking him.

For mile after mile, Robert and his men made their way through the forest, by paths so twisting and secret that few could have followed them. They went through glades and thickets of prickly bush, up and down,

in and out, till at last they reached a great
opening. An enormous oak tree grew in the
centre of the clearing, and on every side the
forest climbed up cliffs of rock. Robin took
out his horn and blew, and men came from
the caves in the rock. All wore Lincoln
green, and all wanted to know what had
brought Robin to them, on his wedding day.
And when they heard what had happened
they clapped him on the back and laughed
and cheered and said they wished that they
had been at the church too.

Later they lit great fires, roasted joints of
the king's deer, and sat down on logs to eat
and drink.

When they had finished, Robin rose to his
feet. "We are all outlaws now," he cried.
"But we are not thieves. No good man need
ever fear us. Perhaps we do steal the king's
deer, but when the king returns we will beg
his pardon. It is so that we may fight for
him that we live by hunting his deer. But
now together we must swear an oath. We

must swear to harm no one who has harmed no other, and never, whatever befalls, to harm a woman. We must swear to fight whatever is evil and cruel, cruel nobles, cruel priests, cruel sheriffs. And our solemnest oath must be to protect the poor, and whoever's been wronged."

Robin and his followers then knelt down, and swore their oath, and then Robin put his horn to his lips and blew that great blast that had seemed to mock Sir Guy as he stood shaking with rage outside the church.

"At the sound of the horn," said Robin, "wherever you are, you will come. It will mean you are needed."

And that is how Robert Fitzooth, Earl of Huntingdon took to the forest under the name of Robin Hood, the most famous outlaw the world has ever known.

2

Robin Hood had some fine fighters in his band. Men who could fight with bows and arrows, or swords, or with a long stout stick called a staff.

Will Scarlett was a good fighting man, and so was Much the miller's son. But one day a new man, who was to be the best of them all, joined Robin.

It happened like this. One morning Robin went off on his own leaving Will Scarlett in charge of the camp. Robin wanted news – news of rich travellers who were on their way through the forest, or news that some poor person had been ill-treated. He watched out for danger, of course. For the

Sheriff of Nottingham had offered a reward for Robin's capture. People were looking for him everywhere, except in the heart of the forest where they dared not go. And Robin knew that in the forest he had only to blow his horn and his men would come to him as fast as they could.

That morning he came to a wide stream, at a place where someone had made a bridge by cutting down a tree and laying it from bank to bank. It was a narrow bridge – only one man could cross it at a time. And on the other side Robin could see an immensely tall man, walking very fast.

"Hm," thought Robin, "he means to get there first. Well, he shan't." And Robin began to walk fast, too.

The tall man came nearer and nearer to the bridge, and so did Robin, and both moved faster and faster, until Robin had his foot upon one end, and the tall man had his foot upon the other.

The tall man cried: "Give way, give way, *little fellow!* I'm in a hurry. You must wait!"

"Oh no," said Robin. "I wait for no *beanpole!* Do you want to be tumbled in the water, you long fellow?"

"It's you who'll be in the water if you step on this bridge," called the tall man. "Out of my way!"

"Well, if that's how it's to be . . ." said Robin, drawing an arrow from his quiver.

"An arrow!" said the tall man. "You would shoot an arrow at a man who carries nothing but a staff! You're a coward, little man."

"A coward!" cried Robin. "No man has ever called me a coward. Wait till I cut myself a staff, and then we'll fight with nothing else."

"Agreed," said the tall man. "In the middle of the bridge."

"In the middle of the bridge," agreed Robin.

Robin took his knife and cut down a young tree. He trimmed off all the twigs, twirled it once or twice in his hands to test the weight, and went to face the tall man in the middle of the bridge.

Then it was all clatter and panting – the noise of staff against staff – a cry from Robin as the tall man broke through his guard – and a crack as the staff hit Robin's head. Robin lurched and slipped, but managed to

keep his balance, and then it was the turn of
the tall man to shout as Robin's staff came
down on his shoulder.

Again Robin took a blow on his head, but
this time he did lose his balance and tumbled
into the stream.

The tall man leaned on his staff and
panted, "Are you in trouble?"

Robin laughed. "I'm in no trouble, long
fellow," he said. "The water's cool after all
that fighting. You beat me fairly – you're a

fine fighter." Then Robin scrambled up the bank. "Where were you off to in such a hurry?" he asked. And as he spoke, Robin took his horn and blew it.

"I was looking for someone who's got your sort of spirit," answered the tall man. "I was looking for the man they call Robin Hood."

At that moment, Will Scarlett and half a dozen other outlaws came out from the trees.

"Robin, you called us," cried Will Scarlett. "You're wet! There's blood on your head! Who is this man?"

"*Robin?*" said the tall man. "Are you . . . Robin Hood?"

"I am," said Robin, laughing. Then he turned to the others. "Put down your weapons," he said. "Unless I'm mistaken, this is a new recruit to our band, and one we'll be pleased to have. If he fights as well with his bow as he fights with his quarterstaff . . ." And Robin looked down at his wet clothes and laughed again. "What's your name, tall fellow?" he asked.

"My name," said the tall man, stretching out his hand to Robin, "my name is John Little and I . . ."

But whatever else he was going to say was lost in laughter.

"John *Little!*" said Will.

"Was ever a name better chosen!" said Robin. "But better still, I think, would be Little John."

"Well, so be it," said the man. "If I'm to lead a new life I shall need a new name."

So it was that the tallest man in Robin Hood's band was ever after known as Little John. And Little John was with Robin on the day he met the Sheriff of Nottingham face to face.

It happened when the Sheriff announced that he would hold an archery contest in Nottingham. All the finest archers were invited; and the one who shot the best would win an arrow with a shaft of pure silver and head and feathers of rich red gold. There would be no other arrow like it in England.

"I'll win that arrow," said Robin, when he heard of it.

"But they'll know you, Robin," said Will Scarlett, "and then how will you escape?"

"With my hood pulled close over my head they'll not know me," replied Robin. "And if by any chance they do, why I shall be there because I'm an archer, and the Sheriff has invited all archers. Even the Sheriff won't harm a guest."

"I'm not sure about that," said Will. "We'll come with you, Robin, in case you're wrong."

So Will and Little John and many other members of the band set out with Robin for Nottingham castle.

All the best archers for miles around were

in Nottingham that day – as well as crowds
of townsfolk and country people. The
Sheriff sat with his own men on a raised
platform at one end of the field to judge
the shooting. It was a gay and lively scene.
Archers in their bright tunics shot at the
target with its rings of white, blue and gold,
watched and cheered by the crowd. There
was the whizz and fizz of an arrow – a
thud when it struck the target – and cries
of praise from the watchers. One by one,

archers missed the target as it was moved further and further away, until only Robin Hood and two other men were left.

So it came to the final round. The big coloured target was taken away, and in its place went a little white stick, so slender you could scarcely see it from the far end of the field.

The first man took careful aim, and the arrow flew. The stick trembled as the arrow flashed past and landed in the ground

beyond. The second archer's arrow touched
the stick with its feathers, but the crowd
groaned as the arrow buried itself in the
earth.

Then came Robin's turn. He barely
seemed to take aim – the arrow flew like the
wind – and the white stick trembled and fell
in two halves as the arrow sliced clean
through it.

There were roars and cheers as Robin
went to the Sheriff to receive the prize. As

Robin fell on his knee in front of the Sheriff, Will Scarlett and Little John watched carefully and moved forward.

"You're a great archer, man in green," the Sheriff said. "Let us know your name. It's a name we shall long remember!"

"My name . . ." said Robin, and looked the Sheriff straight in the face.

For a moment the Sheriff stared in silence, then he spoke. "Your name," he said reaching for his dagger, "your name is Robin Hood! You are over-bold, friend Robin. The fate of an outlaw you know!" He gave a sign, and a man at his side gave a blast on his horn.

"I know what is due to a guest," said Robin. "A guest is free to come and go."

But across the field men came running – the Sheriff's men. Robin felt at his side for his horn and blew it. The Sheriff rose to his feet, pale and angry, and Robin's followers leapt to his side. Then the sound of arrows was heard again – but this time it was no archery contest.

Now it was a real fight to the death. Robin and his men made a little square of green and retreated, firing their arrows. Some of the crowd broke up and fled, but others stayed to cheer – to cheer Robin, not the Sheriff's men. Few of the crowd liked the cruel Sheriff or his men, and many there had been helped by Robin.

"Up with the green and down with the grey!" was the cry, as the crowd scattered.

So fierce and thick flew the arrows that the Sheriff's men had to follow at a careful distance. Many were hit. But one arrow struck Little John in the knee, and he fell.

"Master," he cried, "if ever I was of service to you, now be of service to me! I can go no further. Do not let me fall alive into the Sheriff's hand."

"Little John," said Robin grimly, "I wouldn't have you slain, not for all the gold

in merry England laid in a row." And he
took Little John on his back, and still they
fought their way back to the greenwood.

"Leave me, leave me," cried Little John.
"You'll never reach Sherwood, friends, if you
have to carry me." And it seemed that they
never would; but at that moment through the
trees, the outlaws saw a castle, with a
double ditch round it and a thick, high wall.

"We're saved!" cried Will Scarlett. "That
castle belongs to a knight we helped once

when the Sheriff tried to take his land".

Robin raised his horn and blew, and at the sound the castle drawbridge was lowered. Still firing their arrows, the outlaws made their way across it, and it was drawn up after them.

The Sheriff's men shook their fists and talked of revenge, but in the end they had to leave and make their way back to Nottingham.

Inside the castle, Little John's wound was dressed, and as the outlaws and the knight sat down to a feast, they talked and laughed, and passed the silver arrow from hand to hand, for indeed, there was no arrow to compare with it in the whole of England.

> *A right good arrow he shall have,*
> *The shaft of silver white,*
> *The head and feathers of rich red gold,*
> *In England is none like!*

It was the month of May in Sherwood forest. A time when the hard winter was over and Robin and his men were able to enjoy their outlaw life. They would leap, run, and play games, and have contests to see who could shoot the best.

"Which of you," Robin would cry, "can kill a deer from five hundred feet away?" Many of the men tried, but only Little John could do it.

"There's no better shot in England," said Robin.

"Except you," said Little John.

But Will Scarlett laughed. "There's a friar," he said, "a fine fat priest you'd think was good for nothing except eating and drinking. But he could beat all of you – except Robin."

"Oh, then *there's* someone I must meet," said Robin. "Where does he live?"

"At Eastwood Abbey," said Will. "His name is Brother Michael Tuck."

Then Robin strapped on his broadsword, took his best bow, and went off to Eastwood Abbey. But before he reached it, he came to a stream, and there, walking up and down, was a fine fat friar. He was wearing a friar's brown robe, but he carried a sword and shield as well.

"Good morning, Friar," said Robin. "I wish to cross the stream. You look a stout fellow. Pick me up on your back and take me over. At once, or. . . ." And Robin touched the sword at his side.

The friar said nothing – just looked at him with a twinkling eye. Then he took Robin on his back, carried him over the stream,

and, without a word, put him down on the
other side.

Then the friar spoke for the first time.
'All right, fellow," he said. "Now I wish to
go back to the other side. Pick me up and
take me over. Do it at once or. . . ." And
the friar touched the sword at his side.

So, saying nothing, Robin took the friar
on his back, and trudged with him across
the water. He put him down on the other
side and said: "Well, I still want to cross the
water. So carry me over, Friar, or. . . ."

The friar said nothing, but took Robin on his back again. They came to the middle of the stream – and there, suddenly, he bent forward, gave a flip – and Robin was in the water.

"There you are, fine fellow," said the friar. "Take your choice, sink or swim!" And he crossed to the other side.

Robin swam ashore at once, shook himself, snatched one of the best arrows from his quiver and let fly at the friar. But the friar held up his shield and the arrow struck it. "Carry on shooting, fine fellow," he said. "We've all day, and the sun is shining. I can't think of a better sport."

So Robin shot till his arrows were gone, but all were turned aside by the friar's shield. Then Robin drew his sword and leapt across the stream, and he and the friar fought with sword and shield. They fought all through the long summer day, but they were so well-matched that neither showed

signs of winning.

At last Robin said: "Give me leave to blow a blast on my horn."

"Blow as hard as you wish," said the friar, "and I hope you burst with your blowing."

And Robin blew on his horn, and very soon half a hundred men in green came rushing through the trees.

"I thought there was only one man who could keep me busy so long," said the friar. "You must be Robin Hood!"

"And you're Friar Tuck," said Robin. "You're wasting your time in the Abbey, good friar. We could do with you in the greenwood – as a priest and as a fighter."

"I've thought of joining you often," said the friar, "since you're for King Richard and so am I. I'd gladly come, but. . . ."

"What do you fear?" asked Robin.

"Fear?" said the friar, "there's nothing I fear. But – " and he patted his stomach – "I've often wondered how well you manage to eat and drink in the greenwood."

"Ah, we've nothing to eat," said Robin – and the friar's face grew sad. "Nothing – except the fat deer we kill. Nothing – except joints of venison. It's joints of venison morning noon and night." By now the friar's face was brighter. "And nothing to drink," said Robin, "nothing – except the barrels of ale stored in our caves, our scores of great barrels of ale, and – "

The friar's face was now very bright.

"I'm your man." he said. "Brother Michael of Eastwood I was till this morning – Friar Tuck of Sherwood you can call me now." And off through the forest they all went, laughing.

Not long after Friar Tuck had joined their band, Robin heard that the Bishop of Hereford was travelling through the forest. Not through the *heart* of it of course – no one dared to do that, especially no one as rich as the Bishop. No, he was travelling through the edge of the forest, on his way to Nottingham.

"We'll meet the Bishop," said Robin, "and invite him here to share our meal. And he shall pay for our welcome."

So Robin and six of his men – Friar Tuck among them – dressed up in shepherd's clothes and went off through the forest. On their way they shot a deer, and then they stopped, close to the path the Bishop would take, to make a fire and cook the meat.

Soon enough, along came the Bishop with

his monks and his armed men.

"What's this!" he cried. "That's the king's deer you're cooking! You know that to kill the king's deer is death."

"We're only poor shepherds, My Lord Bishop," said Robin. "We work hard all the year tending our sheep, but today we felt merry and thought we deserved a meal of the king's fat deer."

"What you deserve is a hanging," said the Bishop. "And that's what you'll get from the

Sheriff." He turned to his men. "Take them
and bind them," he said.

"Oh pardon," said Robin, "pardon us, My
Lord Bishop! Surely a man of the Church
will pardon poor men whose only crime
was to be hungry!"

"You can expect no more pardon from me
than you'll have from the Sheriff," said the
Bishop. "Hurry, men, bind them, for we
must be on our way."

Then Robin brought out his horn from

under his shepherd's cloak, blew a loud blast, and almost at once sixty and ten of his men in green burst through the trees. At the sight of them, the Bishop's armed men and his monks made off, leaving the Bishop alone.

"That was a loud blast, Robin," said Will Scarlett. "What is the matter?"

"This is the Bishop of Hereford," said Robin. "We begged his pardon for killing this deer, but alas he could not bring himself to pardon us! What shall we do?"

"An arrow's the best answer for him," said Will Scarlett.

The Bishop turned pale and trembled. "Now, not so hasty, good fellow," said he. "Not so hasty, I beg. If I'd known it was you, Robin Hood, I'd have gone another way. Grant me your pardon and let me go."

"No pardon for you, Lord Bishop," said Robin. "No pardon for you."

"Don't take my life!" cried the Bishop,

falling on his knees.

"No, I won't take your life," said Robin. "That's of small worth, Lord Bishop. But I think in the purses strapped to your side – and those strapped to your horse over there – we'll find something of greater value than the Bishop of Hereford's life. Come, you're condemned. Sentence is passed. You must eat with us tonight – eat of the king's deer, My Lord Bishop! And when we have eaten and drunk enough you shall . . . pay for your meal!"

Then they led the Bishop through the forest. They didn't bother to blindfold him – they knew he would never manage to find the path again. They went through the forest laughing – except of course, the Bishop, who quaked and quivered to find himself in such company.

At last they came to the great opening in the greenwood, and out of the caves came the rest of Robin Hood's men – laughing and shouting at the sight of their guest.

Then they got ready the tables, the logs to sit on, and brought out the barrels of ale. Over the fires that were always burning they cooked the fat deer they had killed that day. As darkness fell, the light of the flames made the trees seem to leap and tumble among their own shadows; the smell was glorious, and Friar Tuck went from fire to fire making sure the meat was cooking properly.

When the feast was ready, everyone took his place ready to enjoy himself – except the Bishop. Sitting next to Robin, he looked dismal indeed.

For hours the feast continued, and the Bishop grew more and more wretched. "Join in our laughing, Bishop," said Robin. "Or is there something wrong with the feast? Is it not quite as good as the feast you'd have had at Nottingham tonight, with our very good friend the Sheriff?"

"I think you must give me my bill," said

the Bishop. "If I'm to pay, you'd better give
it to me now, or I may not have enough to
pay you."

"Well, Bishop," said Little John, "that
would be awkward! Give me your purses and
those from your horse, and I will give you
your bill."

"I'd rather . . ." the Bishop began.

"The purses, Lord Bishop," said Robin, no
longer smiling.

And from all the tables there rose a great
shout: "The purses, Lord Bishop!"

There was nothing the Bishop could do but hand over his purses. Then Little John bowed and said: "And your cloak, Lord Bishop." Little John spread the cloak on the ground and one by one he emptied the purses, spilling the gold until the cloak was almost covered with coins.

"Not enough for your meal, My Lord Bishop?" asked Robin.

"I make it a thousand pounds," said Little John.

"A thousand pounds for a meal!" said the Bishop.

"There are many poor folk who are hungry, My Lord Bishop," said Robin. "Your gold will pay for meals for them. As a good man of the church that will please you, I'm sure."

"And now may I go?" said the Bishop.

"Not yet," said Little John. "You have paid for your supper, My Lord Bishop, but you must sing for it too."

48

"Sing!" cried the Bishop, horrified.

"Yes," said Robin. "All our feasts end with singing, Lord Bishop. We are used to each other's voices – but yours will be new to us. So come, let us have a song!"

The Bishop hadn't a good voice but he sang because there was nothing else he could do.

There was great merriment in the greenwood that night, and it wasn't all at the expense of the Bishop. It was also because of the thought of that heap of gold, and of the food and shelter and protection it would buy for the poor.

Next morning, they took the Bishop back to where they had met him. They put him on his horse and set the animal on the road for Nottingham – but they put him on backwards! And while the Bishop, holding the horse's tail and looking very glum, jolted along backwards to Nottingham, Robin and his men returned along the secret

path to their hideout, laughing.

> *Then Robin Hood brought him through the wood*
> *And caused the music to play,*
> *And he made the Bishop to dance in his boots,*
> *And they set him on's dapple-grey,*
> *And they gave the tail within his hand —*
> *And glad he could so get away!*

4

It was a fine shining morning in Sherwood
forest, and Robin Hood was whistling as he
made his way through it. He was feeling
specially happy because not long before Lady
Marian had slipped away from her father
and come to join him in the forest.

Suddenly he heard someone else whistling.
This was strange – his enemies never
whistled. When the Sheriff and his men
visited Sherwood they came as softly and
secretly as they could, to try to take Robin
by surprise – and to make sure they weren't
taken by surprise themselves. So Robin
went on carefully to the place from which
the whistling seemed to come – and as it

grew louder, he heard a creaking sound,
too. Then, along the path that led to the
clearing where Robin was standing, came
an old slow-moving horse, drawing a cart.
The cart was full of joints of meat, and
behind it, moving as slowly as the horse,
came a fat, jolly-looking butcher, wearing a
striped apron. It was the butcher who was
whistling – so hard that at first he didn't
even see Robin. And when he did catch sight
of the outlaw the butcher stopped
whistling very suddenly.

"I'm only a poor butcher," he cried, in a very worried voice.

"I can see that," said Robin, and smiled. For an idea had come into his head – one that seemed just right for such a sunny morning. "I can see you're a butcher, and I'll take your word for it you're only a poor one. Go on with your whistling – I was enjoying it."

"I don't feel like whistling any more," said the butcher. "And I shan't until you tell me what you want of me. Wearing that colour and carrying that bow at your back, I very much fear that you're an – "

"Sssh," said Robin. "Some words are best not spoken. But you've nothing to fear from me. All I want to know is where you're going."

"I'm on the way to Nottingham to sell my meat," said the butcher. "We've come a long way since daybreak, me and my old horse. I tell you, stranger, I wasn't whistling for fun.

I was whistling to keep my poor old legs going. It's a long road to Nottingham. There's nothing I'd like better than to lie under one of these trees and have a long sleep. But there it is, my meat must be sold."

"Indeed it must," said Robin, "but why go to Nottingham? Sell it to me instead. I'll give you a good price for it, and more still if you lend me the horse and cart and that apron you're wearing."

"He must be mad!" thought the butcher. Aloud he said: "What will you give me, stranger?"

Robin felt in his purse and held out such a handful of silver that the butcher could hardly wait to hand over meat, horse and cart, and apron too! But he remembered to say: "You'll bring back my horse and cart — and apron? I need them for my trade."

"They'll be back here by the time the sun goes down, I promise you," said Robin. But the butcher was already stretched out on the grass, and before you could say "Friar Tuck" he was asleep.

So off went the old horse, trudging on to Nottingham. The cart creaked, and Robin, in the butcher's apron, walked behind, whistling as he went.

The market was busy on that fine morning. There were people selling vegetables, and bread and cloth, and any number of butchers, all calling their wares.

"A fine pound of meat, three pennies a pound," the butchers were calling. A penny was a deal of money in Robin Hood's time. "Three pennies a pound! The very best meat in the market!"

"A fine pound of meat, just *one penny* a pound!" cried Robin. "Come ladies, come buy the best meat! Only one penny a pound!"

"A fine pound of meat for *three* pennies," the other butchers shouted, trying to drown Robin's voice.

But Robin cupped his mouth in his hands and called: "One penny a pound – only one penny a pound for the finest meat!" Of course, all the women hurried to buy their meat from Robin. There was no trade left for the other butchers. Surely, they said, this must be some foolish young fellow who didn't know the right price for things. And if he had money to waste he might be worth knowing. So one of them went to speak to Robin, who by now had sold every scrap of his meat.

"Fine day, young fellow," said the butcher. "Now, look you – all of us butchers are going to dine with the Sheriff. Will you join us?"

"That I will," said Robin, for it fitted in perfectly with his plans.

So Robin and the butchers went off to Nottingham castle to eat and drink with the Sheriff. Before they sat down, one of the butchers whispered in the Sheriff's ear: "We've brought a strange young man with us. He must have money to lose. He was selling meat in the market today for a penny a pound! Think of that!"

"Money to *lose!*" said the Sheriff, and his greedy eyes glittered. "See that he sits next to me at table."

The company hadn't been eating and drinking long before Robin jumped up and cried: "Come, some more wine. Fill the glasses! More meat! I'll foot the bill, whatever it costs."

"He's mad!" said the butchers to one
another. And the Sheriff thought: "He's a
silly young man who's come into money and
means to spend it all. I'll have some of it,
before it's all gone."

Then he turned to Robin. "Good fellow,"
he said, "I hear you sold all your meat this
morning. Now – at home you must have
plenty of fine cattle to sell? To sell at – hum
– a fair price?"

"Yes indeed," said Robin, "indeed I have.
Yes, Master Sheriff, I've two or three

hundred head of cattle. And hundreds of acres of good free land. Come, more wine for the Sheriff! More wine for us all. I'm paying the bill."

The Sheriff rubbed his hands together under the table. "Oh," he thought, "he'll sell his cattle for next to nothing!" Aloud he said: "I'm always looking for good cattle to buy. I should be glad to buy some of yours, if you're selling."

"Well now, Master Sheriff," said Robin. "Nothing would suit me better," and he called for the bill. "Come," he said, "we'll be off at once. Saddle your horse, bring a purse of gold, and we'll be home before night comes."

The Sheriff didn't need telling twice. He called for his horse, and his purse, and off they rode. There was plenty of gold in the purse, but the Sheriff didn't mean to spend any more of it than he needed. They couldn't go very fast, because of the old

horse and cart, but it wasn't long before they came to the edge of Sherwood forest.

The Sheriff turned pale. "Must we go this way?" he asked. "There's a man in the forest called Robin Hood whom I'd – hum – rather not meet."

"Don't worry, Master Sheriff," said Robin, "we haven't far to go. And don't talk of Robin Hood, I beg you. It frightens my horse."

They went on into the greenwood and the

Sheriff grew more frightened still. "Is it much farther?" he asked.

"We're nearly there," said Robin, and at that moment, in a great clearing, they saw a good hundred head of the king's red deer. "There's some of my cattle," said Robin. "How do you like them?"

"*Your* cattle?" the Sheriff cried. "But those are the king's deer!"

Robin laughed. "But they're fine and fat, are they not? Just as I told you. Or would you like to see some more of my – er – cattle?" And he put his horn to his lips and blew a great blast.

"This is not the time or place for joking," said the Sheriff. "Either take me to your home at once, young fellow or – " But at that moment, from behind bushes and trees, came dozens of men in Lincoln green. Will Scarlett and Little John were in the lead, and puffing along at the back came Friar Tuck.

"You called us, Master," said Little John.

"Why, yes," said Robin. "I've brought an important person with me, the Sheriff of Nottingham. He thought he might buy our cattle, but now that he sees them he's changed his mind. That's a great pity, for he brought plenty of money with him, and we should give him a chance to spend it. So let's have a feast, and the Sheriff shall pay. How does that suit you, Master Sheriff?"

The Sheriff had nothing to say. He feared

for his life. But they did him no harm, and when the feast was over, Robin politely took the Sheriff's purse of gold, and sent the trembling man home.

And the butcher? Well, as the sun was about to sink behind the trees, the butcher rubbed his eyes and yawned, and there, in the clearing before him, was his cart; his horse was patiently cropping the grass, and in the cart was his apron. He took them and went home, and never guessed what adventures they had known that day in Nottingham.

> *There are twelve months in all the year,*
> *As I hear many men say,*
> *But the merriest month in all the year*
> *Is the merry month of May.*

For many years Robin and his band lived in Sherwood forest. All that time they were waiting for the return of their true King, Richard the Lionheart. Some people said that the King had now escaped, but few dared to believe the story.

One day Robin Hood and Little John were out in the forest, looking for signs of the Sheriff and his men. They had heard that the Sheriff had gathered many fighting men together, determined to search the forest and hunt Robin down. The two outlaws came to a place where the path divided. Little John went one way, and Robin the other, watchfully. Suddenly

Robin saw a man standing against a tree. He was dressed like a forester, his face hidden by his hood, a bow in his hand.

Robin called: "What are you doing in the forest, friend?"

"I'm trying to find my way," the man replied. "I'm looking for a man called Robin Hood. Do you know of him?"

"That I do," said Robin. "You wish to join him?"

"Ay," said the forester, "I wish to put my bow and my sword at his service."

"If you can use your bow well, and are an enemy of *his* enemies," said Robin, "then I'm sure Robin Hood will welcome you. But Robin takes only the best archers into his service. Will you show me, forester, your skill with your bow?"

"That's fairly asked," said the forester. "What would you have me shoot at?"

"See there?" said Robin, pointing through the trees. "On that big oak tree yonder – a little patch of the bark is gone. Can you hit that spot?"

"Easily done," said the forester. He picked out an arrow, set it to the bow and drew the bowstring tight. "Or a better target, still," he cried, "your heart, Robin Hood?" And with a toss of his head he threw back his hood. It was Robin's old enemy, Sir Guy of Gisborne.

"Sir Guy!" said Robin. "You would kill a man whose hands carry no bow? You – a knight!"

"You are an outlaw," said Sir Guy, "and there is no mercy for outlaws. I swore to the Sheriff that you should die at my hand, and so . . ."

"And so you will stoop to any trick," said Robin. "Then there is no reason why I should not stoop, too . . ." And as he spoke he hurled his staff at Sir Guy, and threw himself face down on the ground. Sir Guy's arrow missed Robin and buried itself in the

bushes. The quarterstaff struck the bow,
smashing it, and Robin leapt to his feet,
sword in hand. Sir Guy drew his own sword,
there was a clash of steel against steel
– Sir Guy drew back, panting – the swords
rose together, glittering in the sunlight,
and then it was all over. Robin was only a
split second faster than his enemy, but that
was enough, and Sir Guy lay dead on the
ground.

Robin wasted no time – for where Sir Guy

was, surely the Sheriff's men were too. And what might have happened to Little John? Quick as thought, Robin took off his hood and tunic; then he took Sir Guy's and put them on. The body he covered with his own clothes. Then he took Sir Guy's horn, blew, and waited.

In no time there was the sound of horses brushing through the trees, voices and the clatter of steel, and into the clearing came the Sheriff and his men. In the midst of them, their hands tied behind their backs, were six of the outlaws, Little John among them.

"Sir Guy, Sir Guy!" cried the Sheriff. "I heard the sound of your horn. You have found Robin Hood? You have taken him prisoner?"

"Better than that," said Robin. "Robin Hood is dead!" And he pointed to the body lying on the grass.

"I promised you any reward you asked

for if you captured or slew him," said the
Sheriff. "What will you have, Sir Guy?
Gold? A castle? Or will you wait till Prince
John can reward you himself?"

"I'll take one of your prisoners as mine,"
said Robin, "that's all the reward I ask."

"A strange reward," said the Sheriff.
"But I know how you hate the outlaws. Take
whichever you want."

Then Robin strode up to the prisoners,
knife in hand as if he meant to kill them on
the spot. But instead, with deft strokes of his

knife, he cut the ropes that bound Little John. As he did it, he threw back his hood. At once, Little John lashed out at the nearest man-at-arms, and as the man staggered, he seized first his sword, then his bow and arrows. Still Robin's knife was flashing up and down as he slashed at the ropes that bound his men. Two more were freed, and had struck down two more of the Sheriff's men, before the Sheriff and the rest of his band had recovered their wits. Then the four outlaws stood side by side and faced their shouting enemies.

"That's Robin Hood!" the Sheriff cried. "Seize him!" But an arrow struck him on the shoulder, and his horse reared and backed away.

Arrows flew in the clearing as the outlaws fought their way backwards towards the shelter of the trees. But soon their arrows were spent, and it was sword against sword – a desperate clash of metal. . . . Could

they escape? There was not a moment
when Robin could reach for his horn and
blow it. It seemed that all was lost.

Then, crashing through the trees, came a
huge black horse; riding on it, a tall knight.
His armour was black, grim black in the
morning sun, and he shouted: "What's this?
Forty against four! Is that fair? Forty
against *five* is better." He spurred his great
horse, and rode into the midst of the Sheriff's
men, his sword flashing. And whether it

was his black armour and his black horse,
or the flashing of that great sword –
whatever the reason – the Sheriff and his
men turned tail and fled; and the black
knight stormed after them. There was
crashing in the forest, a shouting and a
thunder of hoofs – and then silence. Robin
and Little John and the others were left
to free their friends, and to wonder who their
rescuer might have been.

A few days later, towards evening, Robin
again met a stranger in the forest. It was
almost at the same spot, and the man was
dressed like a pilgrim, as though he'd come
back from a visit to the Holy Land. But
after his meeting with Sir Guy of Gisborne,
Robin was taking no chances. His hand was
on his bow as he walked up to the pilgrim.
"And what do you seek in the forest?" he
asked.

"Nothing," the pilgrim said. "Or rather
– I have fought with King Richard in the

Holy Land. Now I'm back in England and seeking friends of our King. I find he has many still. Whether there are some in the forest, I can't be sure."

"But *I* am sure," said Robin. "He has good friends here. I am one – my name is Robin Hood."

"I've heard of you," said the pilgrim. "And I'm glad to meet you. I'd be gladder still to meet your men – all friends of King Richard, I've been told."

"Every man is a friend of the King. And every woman too," said Robin, smiling. "You may come with me – if you swear never to tell Prince John and the Sheriff of Nottingham where we're to be found."

"I swear," said the pilgrim.

So together they made their way through the forest to the clearing where Robin Hood lived with his men. The outlaws crowded round the pilgrim and asked for news of the King. Was he coming back to England at last?

"Yes, I've news of the King," said the pilgrim. "But let us eat first; I'm hungry, after my journey. You shall hear my news after I've eaten."

"Our feast is of . . . deer," said Robin. "Perhaps, as one who has fought with the King, you cannot bring yourself to eat his deer?"

"I'll eat it with as much pleasure as if it were my own," said the pilgrim.

So they had a great feast, there in the

moonlight; and then Robin said: "Come, pilgrim, your news of the King."

But the pilgrim said: "Oh, let's have some games first! After such eating and drinking, let's amuse ourselves. Archery, shall it be, or quarterstaff, or wrestling?"

"Games?" said Robin. "Our favourite game when we've eaten well is the one we call buffets."

"And what is that?" asked the pilgrim.

"It's a game to try your strength," said Robin. "One of us hits you a blow – a buffet. If you stay on your feet, then you hit him a blow in return."

"Good," said the pilgrim. "And who shall be first?"

First was Will Scarlett. He raised his great arm and struck the pilgrim a blow. The pilgrim hardly shook on his feet; he raised his own arm, and there was Will Scarlett flat on the ground, while the outlaws laughed and cheered.

Little John tried next, the tallest and strongest of them all: but the result was the same. And that brought Friar Tuck into the game. Friar Tuck wasn't tall, but he was immensely strong – yet the same thing happened to him.

"Now it's Robin's turn," the outlaws shouted. "You're a strong fellow, pilgrim, but you won't beat Robin." And Robin rolled up his sleeve and struck the pilgrim a mighty blow. This time the pilgrim did shake on his feet, and nearly fell: but he kept his balance, raised his arm . . . and there was Robin Hood sprawling at his feet!

"Pilgrim," said Robin, not even bothering to get up, "you're the strongest of us all. And now you've proved it – what's your news of the King?"

"This," said the pilgrim, and he threw back his hood and showed his full face. "Good news of the King!"

For a moment there was complete silence. Then every man threw back his hood and bared his head. Robin fell on his knees, as did all the outlaws, and Maid Marian came and knelt beside them.

"King Richard!" said Robin. "King Richard – it's you!"

"Yes," said the King. "I am the pilgrim. You've seen me before. I was the Black Knight, too." Then he stared round at the outlaws' camp, at the caves where they lived, at the trees of Sherwood forest under the moon. "My friends," he continued, "you have lived here as outlaws, fighting for my cause. I know my friends now, and I know

my enemies. Your days in the forest are over – I need you. You'll come with me tonight to Nottingham, I've business to do there and shall need your help. But before we leave the forest . . ."

And with a movement of his hand, King Richard called Friar Tuck forward. Then he laid one hand on Robin Hood's shoulder, and the other on Maid Marian's, and he said: "I have heard that you, Robin, and you, Marian, have sworn to be wedded when the King returns. It seems that time has come, so, if your good priest will step forward . . ."

And so Robin and Maid Marian were wedded there under the moon in the forest where they'd lived and fought so long. And when that was done, with the King at their head, they all marched into Nottingham. And the poor people, and the good people, ran out to meet them, but there were others who ran the other way.

The King was great above his cowl
A broad hat on his crown
Right as he were abbot-like
They rode into the town.

In he took good Robin
And all his company:
"Welcome be thou Robin Hood,
Welcome art thou to me.

"And much I thank thee of thy comfort
And of thy courtesy,
And of thy great kindness,
Under the greenwood tree!"